CHIMPS DON'T WEAR GLASSES

LAURA NUMEROFF
CHIMPS DON'T WEAR GLASSES

ILLUSTRATED BY JOE MATHIEU

SCHOLASTIC INC.

NEW YORK   TORONTO   LONDON   AUCKLAND   SYDNEY

Also by Laura Numeroff and Joe Mathieu:
Dogs Don't Wear Sneakers

ISBN 0-590-96974-9

Text copyright © 1995 by Laura Numeroff. Illustrations copyright © 1995 by Joe Mathieu. All rights reserved. Published by Scholastic Inc., 555 Broadway, New York, NY 10012, by arrangement with Simon & Schuster Books for Young Readers, Simon & Schuster Children's Publishing Division. SCHOLASTIC and associated logos are trademarks and/or registered trademarks of Scholastic Inc.

12 11 10 9 8 7 6 5 4 3 2 1   7 8 9/9 0 1 2/0

Printed in the U.S.A.   09

First Scholastic printing, September 1997

For Paul Taylor … with love
—L. N.

To my dear wife, Melanie
—J. M.

And zebras don't cook

And you won't see a kangaroo reading a book.

Horses don't hang glide,

Giraffes don't drive cars
And you won't see a piglet saving pennies in jars.

Mice don't join Boy Scouts

And llamas don't shop

And hamsters don't clean
with a broom or a mop.

Reindeer don't square dance

And seals don't fly kites

And weasels don't travel to see all the sights.

Pandas don't pole vault

And camels don't sing

And you won't find a chipmunk who'll ever be king.

Tigers don't ice-skate
And wolves don't use mugs

And you won't see a puppet show put on by pugs.

Now just close your eyes and draw with your mind.
You might be surprised at what you will find...

Like yaks in tuxedos

And hippos on boats

And otters who ride in parades full of floats.

Or lions who juggle

And squirrels on stilts

And lizards who know how to sew handmade quilts.

Or ferrets who garden

And turtles who dine.

But tell me what you see. It's your dream—not mine!